THE GOLDEN GOOSE

Margaret Hillert

Illustrated by Monica Santa

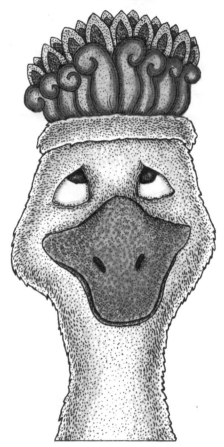

MODERN CURRICULUM PRESS
Cleveland • Toronto

ISBN 0-8136-5051-8   Hardbound

ISBN 0-8136-5551-X   Paperback   14 15 16 17 18 19 20   99 98

You do not look happy, little one.
We want you to look happy.
What can we do for you?
Here is a ball to play with.

3

No, no.
I do not want it.
I do not want to play.

4

Oh, what can we do?
Who will help us?
Who can make you happy?

5

Something is in here.
Something little.
You will see.
Work and you will find it.

6

7

What is it?
What is here?
I will work and work.

9

Down, down it comes.
And look what is in here.
Oh, my.

10

I like you.
I want you to come with me.
Away we go.
Away, away, away.

13

14

Look, Mother.
Do you see what I see?
What is it?
Can you guess?

15

What do you have?
What is that?
We want to see it.

17

Oh, we can not get away.
Help, help.
We do not want to go with you.
We do not like this.

18

Look at this.
Here is work for me.
I have work to do.

19

20

Oh, Father, Father.
Come help us.
You are big.
You can help.

I will help you.
But what is this?
Oh, no!
Now I can not get away.

Go get it.
Go get it for me.
I like to play with you.

Oh, look at Mother.
Look at Father.
Run, run, run.

25

Come away, Mother.
Come away, Father.
Come here to me.
I want you.

I will help you.
I will. I will.

27

Oh, I can not do it.

Here we go.
Look at us go.
Up and up and up.

28

And here we come.

Down.

Down.

Down.

Down.

Down.

Look, Mother.
Look, Father.
Look and see.
Oh, that is funny.

It is funny.
It is. It is.
Now you look happy.
And we are happy, too.

31

The Golden Goose

Margaret Hillert, author of several books in the MCP Beginning-To-Read Series, is a writer, poet, and teacher.

Word List

All of the 57 words used in *The Golden Goose* are listed. Regular verb forms of words already on the list are not listed separately, but the endings are given in parentheses after the word. Numbers refer to the page on which each word first appears.

3	you		a		see	18	get
	do		ball		work		this
	not		play		and	19	at
	look		with		find	21	father
	happy	4	no	10	down		are
	little		I		come(s)		big
	one		it		my	22	but
	we	5	oh	12	like		now
	want		who		me	24	run
	to		will		away	28	up
	what		help		go	30	funny
	can		us	15	mother	31	too
	for		make		guess		
	here	6	something	16	have		
	is		in		that		